MESSAGES FROM GOD
The Complicated Road to Sainthood!

JOHN KAUFMAN

authorHOUSE

AuthorHouse™
1663 Liberty Drive
Bloomington, IN 47403
www.authorhouse.com
Phone: 1 (800) 839-8640

© 2020 John Kaufman. All rights reserved.

No part of this book may be reproduced, stored in a retrieval system, or transmitted by any means without the written permission of the author.

Published by AuthorHouse 12/06/2019

ISBN: 978-1-7283-3906-1 (sc)
ISBN: 978-1-7283-3904-7 (hc)
ISBN: 978-1-7283-3905-4 (e)

Print information available on the last page.

Any people depicted in stock imagery provided by Getty Images are models, and such images are being used for illustrative purposes only.
Certain stock imagery © Getty Images.

This book is printed on acid-free paper.

Because of the dynamic nature of the Internet, any web addresses or links contained in this book may have changed since publication and may no longer be valid. The views expressed in this work are solely those of the author and do not necessarily reflect the views of the publisher, and the publisher hereby disclaims any responsibility for them.

CONTENTS

Dedication vii
Foreword ix

Religious Folklore 1
A Matter of Soul 3
Sensible Shoes 5
Life's Lessons 7
Imagine 9
God's Silence 11
Murmurs Whisper 13
One's Believing 15
Cruel Joke 17
Gut Issues 19
A Soul's Grandeur 21
Lies and Sainthood 23
Early Years 25
Farewell to Teachers 31
Lost Years 35
May the Light 41
Seven Years 43
A Souls Contents 45
Living Commitments 47
End Days 51
God's Children 55
Depression 57
Light 59
Here to Nowhere 61
A Matter of Soul 63
Old Religious Tradition 65
Omnism 67
Theism 69

Atheism	71
Deism	73
Agnosticism	75
Judaism	77
Philosophically Speaking	79
Antiquated Stories	81
The Jesus DNA	83
Breakfast, Lunch, & Dinner	85
Religious Zest	87
Light in Darkness	89
Burdens and Truths	91
Every Season	93
End Trails	95
The Miracle of Benny	97
A Souls Departure	99
Soulless Destination	101
Life is a Journey	103
Therapist	105
Religious Beliefs	107
My Father	109
Reaping What You Sow	111
Only One God	113
Sisters and Friends	115
Judgment	117
The Complicated Road to Sainthood	119
Special Thanks	121
About the Author	123

DEDICATION

I dedicate the miracle of
Benny to all of us who
believe in the power
of our soul.

FOREWORD

In a world filled with depression and sadness, I have stood at life's edge.

Yelling at humanity that I was going to jump to end the madness that was the psychopath world that was ongoing insanity inside my head. I have spent most days of my life listening to the echoes of my father's voice as I stood at life's edge, him yelling at me "Jump nobody cares"!

All those countless times throughout my life, I prayed for God to give me the strength to jump!

RELIGIOUS FOLKLORE

The truth in religious folklore often
defies modern-day logic.
Without faith, doubt will cast dark
shadows on shiny parables!

A MATTER OF SOUL

To think that
a soul can and will
take care of itself
without your participation
will be a soul that God
will take little interest in!

SENSIBLE SHOES

Close your eyes, relax your mind, and imagine having to walk in another person's shoes. Finding yourself living in a world that was, from day one, foreign and far from your perception of what anyone's life should look like!

Twisted, tormented, cold-to-the-touch-like frost on a once warm windowpane!

At this moment in life, when the wickedness of the infinite number of shoes to walk in, you would have no choice in the matter of choosing.

You would spend your entire life trying to understand the shoes which, even before needing them, would never fit, even now!

A world that was so alien to one's sensibilities, you would cry out in pain. Alone, you would suffer through a life-long eternity that left one logically trying to make sense of the stuff that would always remain a mystery.

Just for a brief moment of trying to imagine: "hard for some egos to do," now take a deep breath, let it out, and tell yourself that the randomness of who we all are will let you see who you are! The shoes which you wear were destined to fit or not fit, long before your conception.

LIFE'S LESSONS

I find myself forcibly pushed into this world and then, as now, I found myself afraid of the sounds of life's commotions.

I arrived into the world on June 16, 1950, filled with this same soul-searching turmoil. That friction I had heard inside my mother's womb, these exterior disruptions would eventually plague me with a lifetime of managing my sense of well-beingness.

Those shoes I was born into and the path on which I walked would soon leave me hopelessly in this place I never wanted to be.

Years of dysfunction had left me with no reason to feel safe in a world where one's self-worth lives inside a cracked vessel, and the content of God's creation struggles to have value.

Your maker has not let you down, and it is the soul's need to trust and have faith.

The nurturing of self sometimes is the only way to succeed in believing God never plants a seed without his blessing.

It is the people in our world who will likely let us down!

The accepting of universal truths helps to cushion the soul to the hardest realities of living in this world which lacks honesty, integrity, and the kindness of people.

The randomness of the human spirit does not always make for a beautiful garden.

A man told his friend he had holes in his sock's.
The friend replied, "the Lord has blessed you my friend, all I have left are the tops!" as they watched a man without legs passing by in a wheelchair that did not belong to him!

The lesson in life may not come with the wisdom to know what's more important: you or your soul!

IMAGINE

Imagine the possibility of your life's reflections being the foundation for the beautiful light of your soul, that will serve you well for all eternity!

GOD'S SILENCE

I have spent a considerable amount of time in my life asking God why He had been so silent in a time when messages of his making would be a "godsend" to humanity!

MURMURS WHISPER

I was drawn in, as if to hear the murmurs, always hearing the murmurs, rather perceived, to be voiced with no sound. Quiet voices, in the silent, left only to follow the sacred sounds of murmurs, very clearly and continuously calling, "John."

When you believe you have become an empty vessel, your days will find little joy.
A lack of joy did not stop me from listening!

Without antiquated stories that test a man's enlightenment, there would be nothing to measure "what is of God's making?"

Until your soul is in the presence of God, the source of your distinctions are made so only when you listen to those murmurs—communication from God himself!

When your soul reaches out to you, there will be murmurs and if you are blessed, you will hear God!

A "wannabe Saint" will never hear the murmurs. A Saint is someone who is mesmerized by those murmurs as whispers from God Himself!

Without real logic, everything becomes speculation of a good imagination. A vessel that has become broken and filled with cracks will not hold water and becomes as useless as the murmurs you do not hear!

ONE'S BELIEVING

One's believing can make all things seem possible! While this is not necessarily true, it appears to make us feel better about our convictions to faith.

CRUEL JOKE

On a small dairy farm in Michigan is where the murmurs started. I was born in June of 1950, the third born of several brothers and sisters. June can be a hot month, lots of flies and farmers busy putting hay away for the soon to be winter. It's cold in winter on a farm in Michigan. I never warmed up to the cold. It was the only thing I hated, even now! Hate will kill one's ability to listen for murmurs! My disdain for cold was a blessing, as are my life stories full of murmurs, those whispers that would keep leading me on.

I must confide: I have this God-given ability to remember all. I used to say it was a terrible curse, my life lessons in understanding those murmurs from God.

It has taken me what feels like an eternity to become capable of conquering the understanding of God's speaking to me in murmurs. I am now compelled to share it with you in my writing.

Becoming a Saint is one of divine anointment. However, mostly you must be born in a time and a place of self-recognition of that responsibility. What responsibility might you ask? To be pure of heart.

The world will treat you as it will. But with love, integrity, honesty, truth, and fairness, you need not care about such matters. God's murmurs are all one needs to hear. Many a soul might tell you they have lived a fulfilling and blessed long life; those would not be my words.

My life was far too embattled with staying alive when most of the days, I prayed I would die! It does not matter what is in one's heart and soul when you're overlooked and hold little self-value it would seem. Your mind will become a mass of fear and sadness very early on. I was born into a vacuum of misplaced values. A place that even when I had a lack of thoughts, I thought so! Sharpening my tools, I was always honing my death blade, preparing to be at war with my life, I had no part in its choice. I was born into a desolate, demonic, and bubbling cesspool. But in all my darkness, I too murmured. I yelled, I screamed, and I cried myself to sleep. My distressed cries were my language which had no meaning, which is why I have always, for the most part, been misunderstood.

God's murmurs come in whispers, mine had turned into screams, but even with all my crying out, my murmurs were left unattended. I felt alone and afraid, and I blamed myself. I blamed God, but all I heard were murmurs, murmurs I did not yet understand!

Being the third-born with two older sisters, I was like their rag doll, left to be many times ignored or beguiled with unexplained behaviors. Until I could resist this unacceptable and demeaning behavior, I was helpless to avoid being plopped down on the seat of that three-wheeled tricycle! I was now instinctively gripping the handlebars, holding on as if my life could soon be over! I was gaining speed from my sisters catapulting down the steep hill, not a happy baby.

My three-wheeled chariot was now in full-roll, heading straight for the big ditch at the end of the lawn, which was where the sewage drained. So be it. Most of my days like this would undoubtedly set the tone for most of my life. I left my chariot shortly before my ride ended at the bottom, where I landed immersed in black sticky stank. My life, for me, would always appear blackened with life's endless stank. No matter how I begged for God, if there was one, to please save me from this un-godly place, in which I found myself. He never did stop my endless suffering. Many years later, I would begin to understand why! As it became clear, it was because of his murmurs; I knew I had already been saved, long before I realized any of its meaning.

GUT ISSUES

Even before I could talk, I remember suffering from stomach pain, and it became a lifelong battle. Even now, at nearly seventy years of age, I live on medicines to help with the pain. As a kid of eleven or twelve, my mother was fully aware of my stomach aches. She always kept handy those big pink mints and gave them to me when I was anxious and had a belly ache. The mints were our secret that we kept from my brothers and sisters. It was a gesture filled with the love of my mother!

Validations growing up were seldom heard by any of us, including my mother. My father never said a positive word about any of us, except when using it to hurt someone else, pitting brother against brother. He, without warning, would get upset and rant and rave, yelling how stupid I was, or the times I was accused of having my head stuck up my ass! For the majority of my life, I became trapped in the unending belief that it was true. I was not the sharpest kid in the county. My father would praise how great the other farm kids my age were while belittling me. If he thought it was a way to make me try harder, it never worked!

When the vessel loses its ability to hold water, it will soon be replaced, if only in one's speaking! I was not a vessel my father cherished. I was a throw-away soul, a soul no one listens to, and nobody heard. My screams became murmurs no one understood, including God, it would seem.

Every night, I ended my day filled with sadness, anxiety, and fear of what tomorrow would bring! Over time, the crueler my father was to me, the more I felt worthless, more good-for-nothing. Time after time, I assessed each account to my constant ability to compile all the reasons in the world to be depressed, and pray that God would take me and replace me with someone that my father would value. A worthy enough son that he would not feel the need to knock to the barn floor, as he had done to me. In a rage, he would turn on me, kicking me repeatedly in the crotch, yelling at the top of his lungs, "I will kill you, you good for nothing son of a bitch!" I was only fourteen years old. Where were those murmurs? I had stopped paying attention, and many times the murmurs, it seemed, went away throughout my life. Now, I know the murmurs were always there, and they were from God! When I did not hear them, I had failed to listen.

A SOUL'S GRANDEUR

A soul's grandeur
ultimately relies upon the
light it has been given.

LIES AND SAINTHOOD

I have never told a lie, at least any I can remember. I learned early on in life to dwell in only the truth!

Love and protect your soul's integrity, bring no harm to others, and love totally with the spirit God intended. God's messages led me to know this is true. Thousands of years may come, they may go, but when God himself stood before me, my soul was anointed with his unquestionable and unearthly light. God's murmurs had now become the most beautiful light I have ever witnessed, and those messages were speaking to me. It may seem like this miracle, this blessing for all to hear, is of my imagination! Believe what you will, I have been blessed by God not to have a fear of the message when it comes directly from God.

So many times, I could not understand God's intentions, while so many of the messages were his gift of enlightenment to me.

How could I know that my life would be a vessel, that God would allow me to be a part of such an unbelievable "Holiest of Miracles."

I had finally received what I had asked for so many times. God's modern-day sign of a renewed revival: the importance of our Soul.

EARLY YEARS

My early years contain an infinite amount of memories that I can pick at random, along with the unfolding full-color hard drive in my mind's eye. My ability to remember my life has left me to relive the most unpleasant memories. Most people that know this about me think that it must be an incredible ability to have. I would always tell them it was a curse! The truth is, it is a double-edged sword.

Thoughts from my early years are still vividly remembered even now. Like that summer day, when my dad had been cutting hay, and he came across a nest of baby pheasants. More often than not, they would have been run over by the machinery and killed! They were soon in a temporary wire mesh fenced pen, quickly assembled in the backyard, a sort of birdie corral. Soon, it became a temporary makeshift baby corral for a two-year-old, a three-year-old, and me, their older brother of four something!

I have spent countless long moments where I would become frozen, much like a deer caught in the headlights of an oncoming semi-truck. On this warm summer day with the smell of fresh-cut hay heavy in the air, I found myself pan faced, as I watched in horror at what was now taking place.'

As so many times in the past, I found myself unable to intervene as my little sister had caught one little fluffy-downed pheasant chicks. She had it in her mouth. My younger brother was also ambitiously sucking on a fuzzy little chick's head, as sloppy slime gurgled from the corners of his mouth.

It was as if I was stranded in a time limbo of sorts. I was frozen, waiting for what was to come next. I sat there watching as my younger sister chewed the head off her succulent chicklet. My brother had finally succeeded in sucking the life out of his bird! Holding it in his hand, it was lifeless! He took a moment to stare intently at the dead bird covered with his slimy slobber. He had grown tired of the dead, lifeless pheasant as he hurled it in my direction. I felt a sickening feeling in my gut, feeling the pain in my stomach. I began to cry. There were no murmurs to help me in all those mind altering days, all those years that I felt the sadness of everyday joylessness of life.

Stuck on a dairy farm with nine other people was, at best, discerning to my senses.

I was very timid and shy most of my life, the effects of little to no self-worth. For the most part, it would be a deterrent all my life as I worked hard to not show my lack of confidence.

Without failure, there can be no success; but without success, all that is left is failure!

In the barn, my father could go from silence to a screaming hell-driven madman. He was brilliant in so many ways; he was the best of who he was. When a cow would raise her foot while my father was milking her, knock over the bucket, or worse, get her foot in the bucket, my father would become so agitated he would grab a baseball bat.

Going to the head of his aggravation with the cow locked in her stanchion. He would repeatedly beat her in the head, a maniac who had once again become unhinged!

The cow, bellowing in vain for her life, was eventually knocked off her balance, falling in a twisted heap in her stall. The painful moans of gentle animals tortured by treatment and abuse. The white labored breath shooting from the cow's nostrils in the cold barn air was surreal; she could not escape his wrath. None of us, on that dairy farm, did if the truth is known.

My father, as a young man, was a muskrat trapper. He caught and trapped them for their pelts and the extra money when the ditches and creeks froze over. The young trapper would later solve an annoying problem that occurred daily at milking time. Flies are a nuisance because the barn is full of them, and the cow's tails were forever switching. A wet tail stung whenever it caught you in the face; it was painful and very aggravating to my father.

He solved the problem with the muskrat traps which were no longer used for hunting. It was apparent when people came into the barn wide-eyed, seeing every cow's tail hanging, tightly clamped into a trap which hung from the ceiling behind every cow. However, many times a cow's tail would come out of the trap, which was unacceptable to my dad. Once hit in the face, he would react by aggressively twisting their tails until they were broken in several places. It was a constant reminder of father's cruelty and his lack of anger management when looking at his herd of milking cows with their crooked and knotted tails.

Reminders of the wrath of my father: some cows tails would eventually end up entirely broken off.

Cats are always a part of a farm's inhabitants. My father would not allow more than three cats or less around at any given time. Each time a female cat gave birth to a new batch of kittens, the mother cat would instinctively hide her birthing place. It would only be a matter of time, three or four weeks, when my father would order us to find them. We would always do what he ordered. So, one by one, we handed over each perfect kitten, their eyes barely open. My father, like a well-seasoned professional gunslinger, would, one by one in one quick rotation of their bodies, break their necks and without any emotion, toss them into the gutter, all done with little to no visible feeling. It was a terrible thing to witness, and worse to see them lying motionless. It was such a sad demonic act. Seeing the kittens lying there in the manure gutter, broken and dead, I would cover them with straw, saddened by the assault to my senses!

It was a constant battle between my father and me. I knew he was not very fond of me, never seemingly liking who I was. I would be in my late forties when I understood his love was never available to any of us. Each one of us left to confront the mental manifestations that were taking place within each of us. It was my father's inability to protect us from himself and his world filled with little consciousness or compassion. Years of his creating a family so full of dysfunction and his cruelty of pitting each of us to fight amongst ourselves. Making it clear to our sickening picturesque portrait of a family, my father had constructed it to destroy any love there might have been!

My mother would confide in me, through the years, that my father, after sixty years of marriage, had never told her he loved her. My mother, through my eyes and heart, will always be a Godsend. My mom's world was one of perseverance and patience. She was also codependent on her keeper and survived it always with a happy, positive persona. She was loved, and she had a beautiful and endearing soul.

I never heard God speak during these times of surreal abominations. My father's unhappy demeanor, most days, overshadowed any hope to avoid his wrath. I was always afraid, sad, and full of anxiety. My soul seemed of little importance as there is no "light" in the definition of "dark!" I lived a life of asking God to give me the solace of a better time, and he did just that!

I was, in many ways, unable to construct a guide to interpreting the daily shocking truths and the meanings of much of my life. The disgusting things that took place throughout my life were not about my intellectual perception of them. I could not wrap my brain around much of life's makings, caught in an endless maze with no arrows pointing toward any exit!

I was not yet old enough to start kindergarten, which would come in the fall after summer had passed. It was during this preschool time on a beautiful summer day, my companion and I had wandered off to a wooded area quite some distance from the house. Like any young child, I was unable to lead, so I followed the voice that led me into the bushes. When she succeeded in getting my pants and underpants down around my ankles, I did not notice. I remember her telling me that the kids at school told her, "this is what boys and girls do." As she stood there with her pants now off, she began fiddling with my crotch, pulling and tugging at me. She continued to inform me, as best she could, that my pee-pee was meant to go inside her. She tried ambitiously for a long time to achieve the results of the stories she had heard. I remember it like it was yesterday – her busy attempts to accomplish her task, in spite of my lack of cooperation. I was not interested in her failed attempts to achieve her mission. I was, from the start, more interested in the butterflies and bugs which were flying within my grasp. Her actions were not of any Evil manifestation, and her molestation was never created to cause me any substantial amount of mental anguish. Unfortunately, it was just that! Causation for my mind, which later would be construed to be just that ·total confusion to my ability to process it, still! That day would leave me to start my early years with unanswered questions in understanding what had taken place on that nice summer's day. A day that profoundly changed who I would become. I was not equipped to wrap my mind around the event; I lacked the intellect.

I no longer viewed girls as an alternative pursuit, a girl's vagina, I would conclude, held no interest for me. I was, as it turned out, more interested in the male anatomy or at least in men in general. Growing up on a dairy farm should have been a lesson in procreation. Sex was going on all around me, but I never could gain any insight into this thing called 'attraction' and how it was supposed to work. Never entirely understanding the what, the why, or how come of it all. The years went by, and I now was in the ninth grade. I was invited to go tobogganing with some newly-gained friends from high school. It was during Christmas vacation as I stood in front of the kitchen door anxiously waiting for my first ever date with a girl! I was dressed warmly in winter garb, ready to go on my date with friends. It was a day perfect for sledding at a nearby snow-laden hill, where toboggans frequented during the winter months. As I impatiently waited for my friend to arrive, my father came over and stood uncomfortably close to me. The words that came out of his mouth were utterly mind-altering to me. I was left to ponder what he could have meant when he sternly told me, "if you get her pregnant, you will have to marry her!" I was beside myself, could a person get someone pregnant by an afternoon of tobogganing with friends? It was a harsh warning to me, and I had no power of the mind to comprehend the information I was receiving. It was just another moment in my life, of which I could make no sense!

I don't remember when I stopped hearing God's murmurs; I was too busy fighting off my anxiety, my lack of self-esteem, and my lack to feel I was worth much of anything and that I did not matter, even as I prepared to go to college. I had three younger brothers, and I was never going to be the one to stay and farm. I don't know that I was good at much, including having what it took to be a farmer. My father, as it would turn out, never gave up his control, even when I was trying to adjust to keeping him out of sight and out of mind. He loomed and lurked in my every other thought.

In high school, I met a Christian whose father was a minister of the Baptist church in our small town, and we became the best of friends. I thought the world of her. One Sunday, she asked me to go to church with her, and surprisingly, I did. It was there she explained to me that if I accepted Christ as my savior, I would become a Christian, and for the rest of eternity, I would live forever with the light of the Lord. I received that hope as I was accepting Jesus Christ as my savior, at that moment on that particular day. I received Jesus, knowing very little about the Bible and God's Christians, and not much of what their faith commanded or what they believed. After years of searching for my heart, mind, and soul, I recommend that one should not accept any religious beliefs without contemplation of how it will adorn your soul for eternity.

After four years of my mother telling me to go live with my uncle Jim, I would be the first in my family to go to college.

I worked to achieve several degrees with honors. In hindsight, I did not realize my mother's taunts to live somewhere else was actually her attempt to save me from my father's persecution! At the time, I could see none of the blessings. Even worse, I was being told to go live somewhere else by the woman that showed me love.

FAREWELL TO TEACHERS

Starting with my kindergarten teacher, Mrs. Trowell, she was an essential piece to my entire future as it turned out. I had been blessed early in my life with the ability to excel in the arts. My teaching started with the recognition of the murmurs, and the end message would be a lifetime of being an artist and loving the arts! I have never forgotten her contribution to my life's achievements.

I was never fully present. I kept myself in a sort of dumb existence, created to somehow protect me from having to have the right answers. Every thought was involved with getting through another day.

I have struggled all my life with dyslexia, and reading did not come easy for me. These, along with my other challenges, were never diagnosed or treated. I was alone in my world, and I showed little to no interest in much of it. My disinterest appeared to be because of learning problems or, more simply, I was deemed not to be the sharpest tool in the work shed!

My mother's creativity and artistic blessings fed my creativity. She was a real teacher, unlike Mrs. Nelson, who was my sixth-grade tormentor. Her teaching style was, at best, questionable. Her students, grades K-8th, attended a one-room country school. Her big, oak desk sat up front, positioned to stare at the rows of students facing towards her. Directly across from her desk was a wooden bookshelf where she had placed all the answer books to each grade's workbooks. What was she thinking, that the smart kids needed the answer books, or maybe those less intelligent would adapt to self-help education? What about those few like me? Those of us perceived to be dumb. Was this Miss-what's-her-face's gift to me? Her knowledge that without life's answer book, I would be like a fish without water!

It was the end of the school year, Mrs. Nelson sitting behind her desk, she had called me and said she wanted to speak with me. I nervously walked into the empty schoolroom, where I proceeded up to her desk and gazed at her crooked nose and her unkept red hair. I did not like her. Which surprisingly was the first words out of her, "I know you do not like me!" Frozen, I stood there as she went on to inform me that she was considering to let only my classmates pass on to the sixth grade, but she was sorry she might have to hold me back a year! She was greasing up my frying pan, and the heat was her shaming me into feeling that not liking her was somehow my punishment for me to repeat the fifth grade. She reduced me to begging, and she delighted in making me cringe in my disdain for her as I cried and threw myself into her flame, trying to convince her that I did like her, wailing to please let me go into the sixth grade. I don't remember anything after that!

In the fall, I started sixth grade. Mrs. Nelson had not only passed me, but she had also been replaced with Mrs. Doyle, who would be my teacher for the next two years. I liked this new teacher a lot, and I thought she was a lovely person, even now years later. I was now a teacher with a Bachelor of Art Education degree, teaching Art in a nearby school district, kindergarten through 12th grade. It was at the Elmer school reunion dedicated to all the former students and teachers where I spotted her and waited to get a chance to say hello and catch up a bit. It had been over eight years since the 8th grade and Mrs. Doyle, a teacher of whom I had been so fond, and I finally greeted one another. I excitedly shared with her that I was now a school teacher, blah, blah, blah. As she stood there listening to me, her response was, and I quote, "that surprises me, you were never that bright in school!" I don't remember anything after that.

I was in a relationship with a person and after eight years, we married. She left me eight months later. After eight-plus years, I was not what she wanted, so she left. That was during my first year of teaching, and I wanted so much to do a good job. I was so happy to have the chance, and I buried myself in my goals to educate and teach.

During my first year as the school's new art teacher, I was every female student's crush. I was, what some said, the "best looking guy" in the school. That made sure all the male students disliked me. In the first two years of teaching in this school, I would get the wrath of the school's students. I lived in a trailer home one mile from the school, which made me a close target. My car windows were always being broken out, and my mailbox was also knocked down by students regularly. My driveway would be a dumping place for broken glass and trash repeatedly. One night after dark, I saw my road fill up with the headlights of cars and I could see all these students getting out of their vehicles. It was a mob of students simultaneously yelling" tip over the trailer, tip over the trailer," as the mass of kids ran towards my house trailer.

I immediately opened my front door where I took a stance, along with my twelve-gauge shotgun pointed straight at the oncoming students. I yelled for them to stop, or I would blow their fucking brains out. I held my breath as I stood there, pointing my loaded shotgun at the crowd. When suddenly, the students changed directions, and now the renegade students could not get into their cars quick enough as they made their getaway. I don't remember anything after that, except going inside and turning off the porch light. I had to teach in the morning. That last surprising attack on my senses was months later. It was around midnight, and I awoke hearing sounds coming from outside my house. I went to the front door and turned on the porch light, looking out at my front yard, I soon realized that students had stuck hundreds of those red reflectors that are used to mark the sides of people's driveways. I must have had every red road reflector in the county stuck in my front yard! I turned off the light, went back to bed as I had to teach in the morning.

Things in and around school after two years had changed. I had persevered; I had stayed true to my murmurs of self. I had stayed true to what I had started to do, survive with some glory and self-worth. But I never thought the road would lead me to the last year I would teach in the Peck School System. As the murmurs were telling me after three years, it was again time for life to take me in a different direction.

I had built a robust, successful theater program in those three years. I had filled the gym each year with the annual student art show, thousands of fantastic artists displaying their fine arts and crafts. I had helped the freshmen class build winning floats for the next three years. When for the first time in the school's history, we built our winning Homecoming floats, constructed around a Volkswagen car or the body of the truck, making our floats self-driven, not pulled. All the happiness and excitement I helped create was inspirational for my soul. The love it brought me to witness was the light I so longed for, to feel appreciated.

It was the school's year-end award and honors assembly, after which I had planned to finish cleaning out my desk, as my job there would shortly be over. I had turned in my resignation weeks earlier. I was standing against the auditorium wall along with other teachers, and the room was filled to standing room only. I don't know what my thoughts were during most of the ceremony. I was brought back to reality when they called me to the podium to award me "Teacher of the Year!" I was in shock as the crowded auditorium cheered, clapped, and rose to their feet in my honor. This guy, once considered to be slow-minded and not so bright, was having a hard time absorbing my truths. To receive this prestigious award, a teacher had to have taught for three years, and this was my third year! Some teachers had taught there for decades and did not receive the recognition of my achievements.

LOST YEARS

The lost years were the times that followed. I bought a brand-new Dodge van, spent a few weeks customizing it, and lined with orange carpeting; lots of room for the trip across the country to California to become a guitar-playing songwriting duet. Jimmy Williams, a former student of mine, and myself had for the past couple of years been playing our guitars and singing. We had lots of possibilities to make a name for ourselves. My favorite song was "Nights in White Satin." I loved singing, playing guitar, and writing new music.

Bonnie Starr had been a dear friend of mine with whom I attended high school; we were in the same freshmen class. Bonnie had recently divorced. She was a mom to a four-year-old daughter, a two-year-old son, and a newborn baby boy, Ryan. I nicknamed him "Bummy." It was a happy time in my life.

Nothing could ruin such a beautiful situation, except maybe my father and my Aunt Dorothy, my father's sister, who repeated what my father had told her about my dating a woman with three kids! Her words to me were my father's sentiments in the form of a question: "Why would I want a used pair of shoes, when I could have a brand-new pair of shoes to wear?

If one can have a soul mate, we both knew we had found it in each other. That is as true today as it was fifty-some years ago.

I would leave on a journey to discover who and what I was about!

We both made a decision we needed to do what was best, and because of our murmurs, we both understood. We understood something more profoundly valuable was in this authentic friendship; devotion of a love that has lasted a lifetime and with that came the blessings. The joy of being the recipients of its gifts, is nothing less, nothing more, a perfect union.

My soul mate would go on to meet a great guy, and eventually, they would get married. I was not there; I do not attend weddings or funerals! My father was in attendance; Bonnie will tell you he hugged her and murmured in her ear, "You were supposed to be my daughter in law!" Knowing she had been equated some years earlier as a used pair of shoes, Bonnie had spent plenty of time around the farm. She had seen father's wrath many times, and she knew how he treated each of us through those years.

One day Bonnie had come to visit me at the farm where I had bee helping. As I did not have a job, I was expected to be on the hay wagon and to help milk the cows, both at night and in the morning.

When she caught up to me out behind the barn, the first thing she saw when she looked up was me screaming as loud as I could from the top of the one-hundred-foot silo. As my father was sitting on the tractor below, he heard me yell, "I am going to jump!"

He yelled even louder back at me, as I held on for my life, "JUMP! No one cares."

I don't remember anything after that. Not even how or when I got myself down from that podium in the sky!

I don't know where the time went. It was, I suppose, spent pondering my life's attempts to fill a big, empty hole in my soul. My lack of apparent value to my father would leave me to wonder if it was of God's intent and design. His intentions may have been to have me endure the life of a father who was not concerned about my wellbeing-ness, my mental health issues, or my need for a father's love.

It would be years later when I felt better about our father-son relationship. I had accepted and thought I had understood the murmurs directed at me. It was pretty simple; the fact was that my father never liked me very much! It now made more sense, and it was my explanation to all the others who never seemed to like me very much either. The lesson I learned was also loud and clear, "It's none of my business what other people think about me!"

I listened to murmurs, which eventually led me to walk in shoes on the road to the enlightenment of self-proclamation of one's everlasting soul. That even after all else disappears in the cosmos, our souls will always fill any voids. God's murmurs had shown me so.

My soul needed a father who would love me, and I would be free to love him as well! My emptiness, that void, the thought of being liked by another male was intoxicating for me to imagine.

I was not quick to start wildfires, and would finally decide that being in a relationship was what I felt made me most comfortable. After a short time of living with my first boyfriend, I met Jeff, and he was in love with me. He asked my current boyfriend how he felt about getting out of his way so that Jeff could pursue me. He responded that it would be fine, he is all yours! I was listening to the entire conversation from the hallway.

That became my second relationship with a man, which lasted seven years. Mostly educational years for me, I still felt I was what I had referred to myself as a dumb pig farmer! My uncle Jim was a kind man and a pig farmer. I never wanted to be a farmer: cow, chicken, pig, or otherwise. I would struggle to believe it was not a curse of God's abomination of my particular life. Then, as before, I heard more murmurs that seemed to contradict my curse theory. I was in the second semester at Michigan State University working in the art master's program. I had a Commercial Arts degree, a Bachelor of Art education and soon a Master's Degree in ceramics. Though, I would never accomplish it as plans were made to get to Tucson, Arizona before Thanksgiving Day!

Hate is toxic to one's soul. In the wrong amounts, it can cause many people to commit horrific crimes of self-inflicted persecution! To such an extent, many souls will spend eternity in a dark and empty place.

It was God's message that was clear to me about the thing I disdained so much, the cold! "Thank God from whom all blessings flow," and I owe leaving cold winters of Michigan to Tucson, Arizona as a blessing for me. I began to immerse myself in my new life with a partner who, I would soon start to realize, was turning into a full-blown alcoholic.

I can honestly say I have never been unfaithful to anyone when I was in a relationship. I needed male companionship and wanted to feel worthy of a man's devotion and love. I call these potholes on the road to having a completed soul.

A complete and healthy soul will radiate full of light and glory.

What I knew, for so long perceived to be an evil curse from God and the twisted world he had created for me, were murmurs which would eventually lead me to a different conclusion!

It was six years later when the man I had tried to be happy with was drunk at the local disco club. He informed me that I needed to find another way home as he and Jim the bartender had found common ground; which was the end for us as a couple. However, he would not go far from the shore, as God's twists and turns would change the rest of my life. Those changes would have it endure another seven-years, as I did find a ride home that night.

The bartender unwittingly changed my life because the guy I asked for a ride, became my steady, slow relationship for over the next fourteen years. Seven of which were some of the best years of my life.

During these years, we each lived in separate homes, which seemed to work best for most of those years. I was aware, for the very first time, that the guy I was in love with, loved me as well! At this time, 1980, the supposed wrath of God would show gay men had a price to pay for all the unprotected sex. Bathhouses were leading the way to enable men to have a never-ending rotation of male sex partners. I was never sexually active; I was a virgin until my wedding day at the age of twenty-five. I was not the typical, single gay man. I had a desire for the ritual of dating. Popcorn and a movie, going for a bike ride, and a few hours of good conversation was time well spent.

I had been buying and flipping houses during most of the years Wayne and I were together. He was a sports therapist. We were the image of a perfect couple in the small gay community of Tucson. Many years would go by, seven years to be exact, when we both decided to get HIV tested. It was a good idea for anyone who had been sexually active. Wayne and I were not worried, as we never had sex outside our relationship. A week or so later our initial HIV test results came back.

Wayne and I sat down in the doctor's office where I heard, "John, you are HIV positive and Wayne, you are negative!"

She turned back to me and my deadly diagnosis, telling me how sorry she was. She informed me that I should take care of any loose ends in my life, as the current statistics showed I would be dead in less than two years! I don't remember much after that.

I have a lapse of memory for the next few months. Besides having anxiety over my current dilemma, the most significant change was that Wayne had been germophobic for as long as I had known him! His worst fear now was my threat to his longevity. He could no longer be my shoulder to lean on. He never missed any personal contact after that day when God had once again had shown me, "I must not be of his liking!" I had kept my long list of justifiable notes and memories alive to prove there could be no disillusioned thinking in truth!

MAY THE LIGHT

May the light in each of our souls shine enough for God to take notice!

SEVEN YEARS

In those first seven years, we would spend many weeks on vacation on Maui. For some time, I had not heard murmurs that I could understand. However, on a day trip up hill to Hana on the rainy side of the island and well into our drive up-country, we stopped at a bridge that overlooked a magnificent waterfall cascading down to a sparkling pool filled with the surrounding reflections. I remember so clearly standing on the bridge, mesmerized by the beauty all around me! I was thanking God for the blessing of being able to experience the moment. I was immersed in His creation when I heard a voice telling me to walk over to the end of the bridge.

I could see a steep, muddy, and overgrown slope, looking like others had tried to get to the pool of water below. I stared at the unclear path, reluctant to traverse it. I again heard a command to get down the slopped and slippery muddy hillside. Soon, I stood near the edge of the water which rippled by the falls continuous roar in the rhythmic percussion and motion. I had been there mere seconds when again, I heard the voice edging me to get my feet in the water, which I did. The voice kept commanding that I "go further, to go into further," which I did. The water was now crotch high; at that moment, the sun crested over the top of the falls, creating a sliver of bright rays of light hitting the surface of the water. I followed the sun's rays which had now caused a reflection at the bottom of the pool of water. I looked at what was a bright object, and my brain said, "it was just a soda bottle cap," but I heard the voice telling me, "no, it's not! No, it's not!" Telling me, "I should dive in and get it!" So without much question, I dove into the beautiful bright water and snatched up the shining unidentified object in my hand in one fell swoop.

There is a price of understanding God's murmurs, the price more valuable than the large man's fourteen-karat gold wedding band with the inscription of the wedding date, which was one week from the day I found it under the falls. I can still hear God's commands deep in my photographic soul, and I also still have the gold ring. A treasure that does not belong to me. My gift was my ability to understand the murmurs which I was hearing. They now had turned into messages, miracles of God himself!

A SOULS CONTENTS

A souls contents
should never be
left unattended.

LIVING COMMITMENTS

I have always understood the meaning of commitment. Life for me and my thinking had survived the many years during my search for enlightenment. I never felt in my mind or believed in my heart that no one would be denied the chance to walk each of our chosen paths in hopes that it might lead to enlightenment itself.

My friend Tim from Maui had moved to Tucson in the fall of 2000, where he found work at a local gay bar. I had stopped going out socially a long time ago. I was not surprised when I got a call from Tim to come down, and he would buy me a drink, adding, "oh, there is this guy named Benny that comes in about 6:30 or 7:00 for happy hour. He is always alone and I thought you might like to get to know him."

I reluctantly showed up to say hello to Tim and to meet this Benny guy. I walked into the back-patio bar. There were tables and chairs and a small corner area where a few people were dancing. I walked up to the bar and exchanged greetings with my Maui friend, and then Tim introduced me to the fellow sitting at the end of the bar. Fast-moving murmurs were going through my mind as I walked over to greet this man. Before I shook his hand, I found myself making an oath to God that I was going to be the best friend I could be to this soul. Taking his hand, I was committed to befriending this man I was meeting for the very first time! It should be noted that after I stared into Benny's big brown eyes and held his hand in mine, I said to him, "hey, good lookin", I'm John, it's my pleasure to meet you, buddy!"

I don't recall how we got through those early days. We became good friends very quickly. Soon, we were doing different things together, such as taking his old RV camping to the Gila River, or my helping him around his house with chores he was unable to do. I was inspired to help Benny whenever I could. He realized who I was in the matter of Benny. I was his only friend, his hope, and his light, and the blessings were given abundantly to us both! Each day, I worked at performing my daily miracles, I just knew I could resurrect my friend from death's grip. The moment I met Benny, I had made a lifetime commitment to a very sick man who was slowly losing his battle with AIDS.

I had decided we should take a big adventurous trip while Benny was still able. We chose to spend a week at Club Med in Cancun, Mexico, on its annual one-week, all-inclusive gay week. We were both excited, and I was happy to cater to Benny like his private nursemaid, helping him walk, or many times, I would push him in a wheelchair. Three times a day, I would get us to the dining room and to a table, where I would then get us two plates of food and our drinks. We had such a great time, and I loved seeing Benny living life. He always seemed oblivious to everything unpleasant, maintaining his constant happy nature! Each night, we both went to bed early, and I kept his schedule as there were things we wanted to do! One of which was a guided bus tour that traveled to the nearby Mayan Ruins about two hours from Cancun.

Our most significant accomplishment was when, with my help, Benny and I made it to the top of one of the tallest ruins. Our travels were now filled with so many memories, blessings, and photos to take back home to treasure. The week slipped by, the friends we had made called me "St. John" and I wanted to believe it was true!

Back at home, it was not long before Benny soon developed valley fever. This particular type of bacteria remains dormant in the desert soil until it is disturbed and a person breathes in the sickening bacteria. Valley fever was the worst thing he could endure. At this point, the bacterial fungus was rapidly taking over his body. His lack of immune function and all of the other opportunistic battles Benny had been fighting soon had him in a hospital bed. Hooked up to a drip line several hours a day, he took it all as only Benny could, good-natured with a smile.

Benny was losing his battle to AIDS! I was now learning that all my commitments and divine interventions, were not as divined as I had prayed they would be. I was not capable of performing such Godly a task. I was staying full time at his house and sleeping in the front bedroom. Benny slept in the living room where his hospital bed was set up.

I was his full-time care provider, and he also had a visiting healthcare nurse stopping by twice a week or when he needed urgent care.

Benny had shown me photos of himself when he was a big man of 295 lbs. He was once a riding and roping cowboy, and now he was a frail 60 lbs. His skin draped over his emaciated skeletal frame of a once vibrant human being. Now, I spent hours tending to his needs. He suffered from terrible bedsores. I discovered if I rolled him on his side and duck-taped a hairdryer to a chair, I could set it on a gentle air cycle that kept the painful sores dry so they could heal.

Benny was always a happy, spirited individual as he was his last night before he would surrender his last breath the following morning. It was a miracle, as I try to formulate the words that describe knowing that Benny had been impatiently waiting for me to hear his murmurs to wake me up! God does work in mysterious ways, as I found myself anointed with Benny's eternal soul's departure.

END DAYS

It was, for Benny, the end of days here on earth as he quietly laid there, slipping from life's grasp. It was on this last night that my sister offered to spend the night over at Benny's, as she was very much concerned about how I would handle Benny's passing when it occurred.

Gayle is and always has been a blessing and a real gift from God to me. My three apostles are made up of my hallowed mother Marion, Gayle, my oldest sister, and Bonnie, my dearest friend. I will always be present to the blessings and gifts they brought to my soul, each of them a miracle of God's workings.

I had called Benny's father late that night to inform him that Benny was inching near death. His father's reply was, "oh, he will be ok! I will come to see him sometime in the morning," then he hung up the phone.

Benny's father had, early-on, referred to me as his "first grunt!" I had learned it was a term used to describe me. The newly-anointed cook, dishwasher, and Anglo gay man who found himself displaced in the middle of a large extended Hispanic- speaking family! Their Mexican souls were culturally not indigenous to my understanding of them as a people – making me question any self-enlightenment in the attention to the light of their souls.

It was now two o'clock early Sunday morning; Gayle had just gone into the spare bedroom to lie down. I checked on Benny, which I always did before turning off the lights, then went to lie down myself in the master bedroom. I quickly fell asleep. I had no idea how long I had been sleeping when I suddenly sat up in bed!

"Oh, dear God, Benny?"

As I hurried into the living room, I stopped and stood approximately five feet from the foot of his hospital bed. Adjusting my eyes in the early morning dim-lit living room, I was focusing on where his head should have been, but I only saw his legs! Soon, I could see he was sitting on the top of his inclined hospital beds headboard! When my eyes focused on his face, my eyes met his eyes, two hypnotic shafts of light shot out of his pupils, locking our eyes together. Then he opened his mouth. I was moved back physically! When the most brilliant, holiest of light shot out of his opened mouth, striking me in the chest.

My heart racing, I became breathless as, in the absolute silence, I heard telepathically, "it's about time you got up, I have been waiting for you!"

I stood there looking at Benny sitting atop of his hospital bed, my eyes witnessing his aura being of unearthly beauty in his perfection. He was happy, he was healthy, and he was full of the light of God's intention. In that brief time, those precious moments with the incredible image of my friend's soul etched in my mind, Benny, sown by God's seed, had ascended before my eyes.

It was as if time and space had stopped, and I now was in full awareness as I ran over to Benny's bedside and felt no heartbeat or breath. I instinctively put my hand on his catheter bag, which still felt warm, adding to my assurances he had been waiting for me!

I immediately woke up my sister Gayle, and then I called Benny's father to let him know that his son had passed, the time was 5:30 Sunday morning! My second call was to 911, "Hello, what is your emergency?" the lady asked me. I responded to the question, "my friend has just passed away!" I was quickly asked if I would start CPR on my friend? My response was, "No, it would serve no purpose to Benny now!"

I had been standing for hours by Benny's side keeping his mouth and eyelids closed with my hand, as the entire extended family began to show up and began to march by Benny, with me at his bedside in my tee-shirt and boxer shorts that I wore to bed, not so many hours ago. I stood by Benny's lifeless body as all his cousins, uncles, aunts, sisters, brothers, nieces, and nephews were showing up to give their last respects. Each one of them saying a prayer over Benny's soulless, empty vessel. Its contents were worthy of God's delighted and joyful blessings of his departed soul where it would shine for eternity.

I kept watching over Benny as I waited for the people who would soon be here to take Benny's body away for its cremation. The house was now overflowing as people moved together in the backyard. It seemed like hours that I had been standing by Benny's side when finally, two men showed up in an old van to take his remains away. I was privileged to be the one to get Benny's lifeless body onto the gurney. Then, I completed my final task for my dear friend Benny. I was now pushing him out on his last chariot ride, which was soon pulling out of the driveway as I stood there with big tears running down my sad and tired face.

I don't remember walking into the house where this somber day had become a celebration of Benny! The Mexican beer was cold and plentiful, while bags of Mexican food had miraculously arrived as I could see it on the counter next to the stove. As I tried to form some cohesive reality of my current situation, I became overshadowed with Benny's father pointing his finger towards the kitchen. Where he quickly let me know that "I was still the first grunt around here, and I better get in the kitchen and cook these people some breakfast!"

Weeks later, I would speak at Benny's memorial service. Seventy-five to one hundred Hispanic faces were in attendance, steeped in their cultural heritage when death comes to call! I would deliver my truth to them, the miracle of Benny's passing, it was a moving bunch of words! God inspired the sermon that I gave with all my heart and soul that morning. I had overlooked one minor detail: most of those attending the memorial service did not speak or understand English. I was one of the few to speak, and the attending guest politely listened while I spoke in my foreign language.

Once again, the messages from God's work require me to tell the truths in my soul's quest to become a "Saintly messenger of God!" A soul filled with his light, the victorious glory, and I believe He has deemed me worthy of such blessings.

I believe that God's murmurs to me were as He intended. Why am I now planting the seeds of thought and thinking of God's connection to your soul? Because of the murmurs, the messages, his miracles, and the blessing of Benny for me to witness with my own eyes, God's eternal holiest of light. I stood witness to God's enormous bountiful love, His connection to the hereafter! His light has no measure, as it is infinite by design. The stories of God told in the past are not of holy making! Wrath requires qualities that He does not process. It is instead the wrath of those filled with darkness and vengeance. Those of us who are most guilty of selling our soul whenever it would seem the most useful thing to do at the time, while never considering the harm done to a soul's eternal light, that, over time, will become cloaked in nothing but useless darkness.

My epiphanies, as one might expect, have profoundly changed me, the logic of God's love is all-inclusive. We are all, each and everyone, a profound individual seed planted by one God. Just as each soul is a testament to God's intent, He alone will decide if your soul is worthy of his divine attention for eternity!

GOD'S CHILDREN

All of God's children come ready to be filled with light, love, and the holy spirit. God is not of any darkness, and your soul only thrives in the light!

DEPRESSION

Depression? I would one day learn I was a poster child for this terrible mental infliction.

I began to reap the effects shortly after birth and it is a condition created when one's "soul health" reflects a life that is totally out of Katti-wank. It leads you to places your soul, that was born of God's light, will begin to spend days in dark places of one's beingness!

Life's elements are painfully affecting one's mind and body, and that is a natural transgression of aging. In death, our suffering ceases by God's natural law of birth, life, and then death. "Dust to dust, ashes to ashes," the soul is now free to the blessings of an eternal hereafter.

Angels Don't Have Wings!

The best nurse I could have prayed for was Gloria, who worked alongside Dr. Darragh. Both of them were my primary caregivers for over thirty years. Gloria had long ago seen the sadness in my eyes, always full of my misguided thinking about my life. All those years of feeling had made me sick for the last sixty-seven years. I have many times taken a mirage of prescribed anti-depression medications, starting in my mid-twenties. I eventually was prescribed meds that I still take daily, forty years later.

Sometimes it seemed to help, while other times, my anxiety would keep me agitated by what some might say was my irrational thinking and my fears. Most fears are irrational to everyone except the one who is fearful!

It is evident through the years of looking at family photos. Even in my happiest of poses, I was not. It was for the camera, and the response to the commands to, "smile, say cheese!"

My lack of self-esteem and anxiety had created years of stomach problems, making me feel like an ancient soul of God's design.

All those days had slipped away. Going through each day of life, questioning God's blessings! His miracles in the murmurs, which eventually led me to be graced by his holy presence. On that hallowed day, God gifted me to witness the truth of eternal life, "the hereafter." The day Benny died, God revealed to me the miracle of a dying man and his soul's departure.

God's message regarding the resurrection of one's soul requires you not merely live with heavenly convictions, rather be of them.

LIGHT

May the light of your
soul shine enough for
God to take notice.

HERE TO NOWHERE

Old looking young men, hot but cold and church steps are going nowhere, nowhere.

Who am I? Only nothing! Here I am something, but that equals nothing somewhere else or nowhere else, whatever the case may be.

Old looking young men just looking, hot and cold feeling kind of warm and church steps going nowhere, nowhere!

Who are you? Something somewhere, but equals nothing if you don't know where somewhere is and even if somewhere is somehow here, it's nothing nowhere or somehow nothing somewhere.

Cigarette machines that don't give you your cigarettes, feeling happy or sad, I mean sad or happy, or rather, just feeling OK!

Besides, where does it get a guy, but nowhere, nowhere!

Just a big hand in the sky, which equals something somewhere, but somehow equals nothing nowhere or somewhere equaling one big nothing right here!

But if that's the case it's something somehow right here, not nothing, not something, just not!

Just two nothings or somethings, equaling something or nothing, somehow, somewhere, whatever the case may be!

J. Kaufman 1972

A MATTER OF SOUL

2019-2020
Current world population!
7,725,581,399

Births this year!
87,023,086

There are more than 900 million Protestants worldwide, among them, approximately 2.4 billion Christians.

Globally there are 450-500 million atheists and Agnostic worldwide.

China has the most with over 200 million professing to be Atheists.

By 2050, the Christian population is expected to exceed 3 billion.

Each one of us, regardless of inspiration, has one fundamental connectional trait: we each process a soul.

OLD RELIGIOUS TRADITION

Volumes of ancient and old Religious traditions are being passed down generation after generation, family after family! Relics from man's fabrications in past times where logic had little influence on the thinking.

OMNISM

The belief that no religion is the only truth, rather truths can be found in all religions!

The term was first used in 1839 by poet Philip J. Bailey "I am an Omnist, and believe in all religions."

THEISM

Theists believed there is at least one God.

ATHEISM

An Atheist is a person who rejects beliefs that any deities exist.

DEISM

Deists consider themselves to be disciples and students of Jesus because Jesus taught the natural laws of God. Christian Deists believe Jesus was human.

AGNOSTICISM

It is the idea that the question of the existence of God has no coherent and ambiguous definition.

JUDAISM

The ethnic religion of the Jewish people. It is an ancient, monotheistic Abrahamic religion with the Torah as its original fundamental text.

PHILOSOPHICALLY SPEAKING

Be aware that the soul will always take notice of what you are, it is what you believe!

Life's most challenging dilemmas regarding choice are one's inability to choose!

A soul's contents should never be left unattended.
It relies on you for its inspiration and well-beingness.

Until your soul is in the presence of God, the source of your blessings could be misplaced.

To be of the thinking, "the soul can and will take care of itself without your participation," will amount to the soul in which God takes little interest!

Be blessed in the light that speaking outside the negative will begin to produce!

J. Kaufman 2019

ANTIQUATED STORIES

Without antiquated stories that test man's enlightenment, there would be nothing to measure what is of God's makings!

THE JESUS DNA

God has led me to many truths and falsehoods those lies told in a confusing world of two thousand years of endless religious beliefs.

My logic tells me there is one God who has given humanity a wide range of creative interpretations within each of our souls!

Logic tells me when a body dies, only the soul departs, and the dead flesh remains left behind for us to dispose of properly!

I was a witness to Benny's departing soul, and he was spectacularly perfect in every way! He glowed with a healthy, vibrant, and happy aura! His ascending soul's departure, as his body cloaked in death, laid there in the hospital bed below.

I think Jesus would mimic that death and His departure,
just as I witnessed with Benny's passing.

I believe in the scenario Jesus did die; his soul would depart upon his death. With his soul ascended, his body would soon begin to decay, and time would be of the essence to dispose of Jesus's remains.

If he did survive his crucifixion, secretly he would have had to retreat into hiding, which is what many historians, researchers, and scholars believe. They follow the trail which led them to France where Jesus and Mary Magdalene were married, and together, they had two daughters. Fascinating, some conjecture that the DNA of Jesus Christ is here among the living.

The Catholic Church hunted down and slaughtered anyone speaking of such discretion to the church's beliefs and doctrines. Not to mention their control over all those who joined the church. A decision they made based on the belief, the assumption, that Jesus had died on the cross and believed he was the only begotten son of God! Any other portrayal of Jesus' death would discredit any truths in the Bible's scriptures that went with this father, son, and holy ghost assumption.

I don't believe God has any objections to thinking logically.

I saw a movie about the life of Christ. It had been three days after he had risen. In this betrayal, Jesus returns to be with his disciples; they were all in awe of his reappearance.

He assured them he had risen from his death on the cross. Jesus eventually asked if there was something to eat, portraying him to be hungry. A plate of food was quickly brought before him of which he ate!

BREAKFAST, LUNCH, & DINNER

Angels do not need wings and they don't eat breakfast, lunch, or dinner, and neither did Jesus after his death!

God is the focal point here, not the time of Jesus's death. Whenever he died, he did not take with him his flesh, his blood, or his lifeless body. He, just as Benny had done, departed with a soul worthy of God's grace and acceptance.

Some are trying to trace Jesus and Mary Magdalene's genetic ancestral DNA from the two daughters they are rumored to have had! Though it is unlikely, having distant relatives of Jesus living in today's world is undoubtedly plausible.

Losing faith is not the answer that will lead you to enlightenment when it comes to what to believe or what not to believe.

The secrets of what some believed to be truth are hidden in messages, depicted in many of Leonardo da Vinci's paintings. Look at many of the hand and finger positions. The fingers are uncomfortably spread, forming an "M" sign. A secret message to those who knew the truth, but feared to speak about it!

RELIGIOUS ZEST

Throughout history, there have been those who have desperately tried to control their people's beliefs and customs. The Catholics were an influential force in maintaining any rumors and religious beliefs everywhere they went. They decimated entire cultures in the madness of their lack of foresight and respect. Not many could stand-up against their zestful religious pillaging. No one dared to challenge the "Heaven and Hell" doctrine or pay with their lives. Death was the price of deviance!

Does any truth or falsehood matter when it comes to religious beliefs? I will tell you this truth. There is only one God. Anything less or more requires you to doubt your commitment to God the Almighty.

Within many of God's messages, I was comforted by his acknowledgment to truths and untruths in the Holy Scriptures!

Many of the religious stories believed to be the gospel truth are not. Many scholars believe they have been embellished by those who wrote them.

Conscious Choice's

What you choose to believe is conscious self-design. Your soul is your unconsciousness, which may serve no one if it does not become the focal point of your life's continual nurturing.

LIGHT IN DARKNESS

Dark! Not a sliver of light,
soft as heaven, dark as night.

I am lying in a place no bigger than I!
Oh Dear God, I'm not dead, I didn't die!

But what is death, and where do you lie?
Just in times grip the same as I!

Each will live as each will die; the light in a nurtured soul
will shine eternally forever!

BURDENS AND TRUTHS

How have I changed since God's miraculous witnessing of Benny's death and the witness to his resurrection?

The witness allowed me to hear God, seeing that His intentions are of love. God has no wrath; it is you and the bad choices you make which show up as darkness in one's soul.

The devil's wrath is the maddening cry of the man himself, and God is the only way to a soul obtaining the chance to have everlasting life. Benny was proof of the perfection of his soul; God accepted him because he was a glorious flower in God's kingdom!

Angels don't have wings!

I am sorry to paint my portrayal of the made-up! Our Ancestral ability is to be overly creative and have unrealistic interpretations of religious stories, paintings, and fables that contain no logic!

Why is it that history presents itself as factually inaccurate? The mystic beliefs of countless souls, who knew so much, though not enough for God to Notice?

There is only one God, and He is the seed in the soul's
individual making! He is many things to many people. To some nothing, to others, he is all.

All of God's children come filled with light, love, and the holy spirit. The holy spirit does not look for the darkness;
all that is of value is your light.

When one has died, we are left to dispose of the body; the remains after death are useless!

For Jesus, it would be no different! I don't believe he arose after his crucifixion because he did not die. And if he did die, his soul surely went to be with his maker and his body would have to have been earthbound, left to the attention of the living. Then, for nature to be the mortician attending to its final destination.

EVERY SEASON

When in the winds of days gone by, the message is clear: it is not the nature of God to disempower any soul that He is responsible for creating.

It would be like God harvesting what he had planted before it would bear any miracles, which is God's nurturing intention.

When there is aggression in opposition to other religious beliefs, God does not stop you from your earthly battles against one another. Instead, He will see your soul as lacking in the qualities, not of God's making but man's!

May these words bring humanity closer to God's connection with every soul.

Learn a second language, the one your soul waits for you to speak.

Be blessed in the light that speaking without being cynical will produce. The soul longs for your compassionate participation to survive what God has blessed each of us to have.

J. Kaufman 2019

END TRAILS

I have struggled with choosing which words that are here to read, as my intentions are honorable and heartfelt about the conversation of enlightenment and one's soul. All else will fall ultimately to the hands of destiny.

When the importance of the soul is lost in humanity's value, then, as countless of souls gone before us, they have taken little time tending "their souls" of which God had planted!

God's intention is our success; He is most glorious when each of us becomes a gift of God's purposes!

When God commanded that I should witness Benny's departing soul, what I saw was a healthy, happy man of a joyful spirit. He was this perfect soul, entering what has long been known to be Heaven.

Benny is a modern miracle!

I have often wondered if the many gifts of stories in early biblical writings were mandated by God or by man.

The infringements were taken with the human need to create answers to questions of death and mortality that needed to have answers.

I have been anointed by God to be a witness of the most spiritual of matters: life, death, and the soul's departure!

THE MIRACLE OF BENNY

The miracle of "Benny" was of God's creation, and it was the answer for which I had searched. Benny's death was my holiest of earthly moments when God revealed his presence to me.

A Question of Change

How have I changed since God's miraculous witnessing of Benny's passing and the witness to his resurrection?

The witness allowed me to hear God and see His intentions are of love. God has no wrath; it is you and the bad choices you make, which show up as darkness in your soul.

The devil's wrath is the maddening cry of man, himself, and God is the only way for a soul to obtain a chance to have everlasting life.

Benny's miracle was proof of the perfection of his soul; God accepted him and he is now a glorious soul in God's kingdom!

Benny, in God's eyes, was neither straight nor gay, black nor white! He was uncomplicatedly glorious.

God only sees the love in our soul, who and how we love is of little consequence.

Angels don't have wings!

A SOULS DEPARTURE

I have little concern about the logic that in my portrayal, so much was merely made up! Our Ancestral reporters were inspired to be overly creative. The storyteller's dilemma allows his imagination to embellish unrealistic interpretation of religious stories, paintings, and fables that contain no logic!

Why is it that history presents itself as factually inaccurate? The mystic believes in countless souls who knew so much, though not enough for God to notice!
All of God's children come into this life filled with a soul ready to absorb your light and your darkness.

When one has died, it is the living who are left behind to dispose of the body. A human's remains after death are like the butterfly's cocoon, which he leaves behind in exchange for his wings.

For Jesus, it would be no different!

I don't believe he arose after the crucifixion, because I think he did not die as Christians writing teach. At the time of his death,' whenever that time was, his soul departed to meet his maker. Jesus' lifeless body was left to the immediate attention of others.

God created natural laws of the universe; death and decay are part of the body's journey.

SOULLESS DESTINATION

No one can avoid
the consequences
of a soul wandering
around for an eternity
without a destination!

LIFE IS A JOURNEY

Wherever you go, your soul has no choice but to follow. The direction you go is crucial to its survival.

Permit yourself the time to soul search, to question whether your soul has become a garden or a garbage dump for your life.

One's life may past in countless ways, and a well-attended, weed-less soul shall rise to the perfection of which God had intended.

THERAPIST

Having spoken to therapists throughout the years, I found one professional's remarks about "family" as memorable and valuable!

She proclaimed joyfully, "I have a wonderful loving family; I just don't happen to be related to any of them!"

All those times I thought by hiding out of view, little did I know my behavior only made me stand out!

John Kaufman

RELIGIOUS BELIEFS

Religious beliefs and practices are choices made by the living. God does not participate in such personal discrepancies of choice!

MY FATHER

My father, as a young man, enlisted in the Army. He was joining thousands of other men who were bravely signing up to fight in World War II. But after his military physical, he was informed he had heart problems and was not healthy enough to serve his country. He was told to go back home. He had maybe two years to live. I understand how that prediction of a two-year life expectancy can alter one's thinking. I had been given that exact prognosis in those early days: to go home, take care of business, and prepare for death.

My father lived to be 84, that's when his heart finally failed, he died instantly. Many times, when in the barn, during one of his anger episodes, he would collapse down against the barn wall, grabbing his chest gasping for air! In between his dying breaths, he would repeatedly grumble, "you're killing me, you're killing me," as we watched in horror! I don't remember anything beyond that picture of him etched in my mind.

My dad was a complicated man who seems to have forgotten about his everlasting soul. He was a talented and successful farmer. From his crops to his highly awarded dairy production awards, he successfully created much of his wealth by starting a bull semen ring. He was of strict German heritage and, seemingly, his DNA wanted perfection. Unfortunately, none of us ever were, and that alone kept his bipolar rages happening daily. Even on days that he didn't act out of anger, his discouraging words of demeaning language were relentless year after year after year!

Toxic to each of our delicate souls, the toxicity, that started from day one, destroyed any hope for joy in the family. To this day nothing has ever changed - a family filled with ongoing, corrosively-filled mental illness, which seems to have inflicted all of us.

You reap what you sow, and my family was then, as now, a vile creation of the soul that keeps us all driving the tractor fueled by dysfunction!

My brother Jim said in regards to his love for our father, "If I were on a tractor, and Dad got in front of me. I would run him over, and if I looked back and saw him getting up, I would throw it in reverse and run over him again!"

Evil is contagious and becomes a sickness of one's soul.

My father, in life, had a will, which he changed periodically upon his fondness of those included in his most current will.

Upon my father's death, his most-recent last will would leave one daughter, along with my brother and me, nothing. That was another battle he had left us to fight, to find a different conclusion. His wishes upon death were that his remains go to Michigan State University's Medical Cadaver Program. He always thought he would be useful even in the end!

Three years later, his ashes returned to my mom, who lovingly kept them in an urn in her living room.

There were no memorials for my father or mother after they had passed.

The entire disconnected family, having been driven by mental dysfunction, has taken us to a place where we have little to no regard for one another.

My dad could shock and awe me in ways only my father could. Later in my life, I was having a conversation with him about all the hundreds of letters, gifts, and cards I had continuously sent over the past forty years. Without missing a beat, he looked at me and replied, "You should have saved your postage!" I don't remember much after that in regard to the conversation. However, it would lead me to ponder whether many times in my life my love and my intentions ever produced any happiness or joy in a man's soul that lacked both.

I have no room in my soul to have it filled with someone else's convictions to un-enlightened darkness!

REAPING WHAT YOU SOW

The words in my message presented here should not be misconstrued to be about religion. I believe God's connection is the light in the soul's content; all that was long ago is trivial.

If I have offended any peoples, religions, or the beliefs of any individual, it was never my intention.

My only intention was to tell my life's story and share the miracles in my life. To share my story of Benny's soul's departure and what it means to us, the living.

If I have succeeded, it will be the dawn of a better day. For you, your soul, and your connection to the hereafter.

May your life reflect its brilliance through a soul that can only reap the light it has been given to witness!

ONLY ONE GOD

There is only one God and He is of the seed in the soul's individual making! He is many things to many people, to some nothing, to others he is everything.

SISTERS AND FRIENDS

I was especially blessed all my life to have Gayle, my sister, and Bonnie, my forever friend, paying attention to me.

The two of you have always been gifts of God!

Mom was always, and will always be a beautiful soul.

John

JUDGMENT

Judgment is not the job of mere mortals such as ourselves,
Because your soul will become like you, filled with narcissistic arrogance!

THE COMPLICATED ROAD TO SAINTHOOD

Through a lifetime of being confused, living as best I could in this world that is so full of hostility and discontentment, God must also be dismayed and saddened by the bad seeds which have taken over the world that He hath created!

As for me, I am living each day, each week, and each month, feeling happy most days.

When asked how am I feeling, I reply with laughter, "old!"

I have endured my walk through life with shoes that were not of my design, that would never change; it was what it was!

In my later years, I have learned to manage myself the best I can. Anxiety, along with enlightenment, tends to make the illogical seem silly in hindsight, and my hindsight has allowed me to see that God's murmurs were simply blessings, which led me to the miracle of Benny.

It's a complicated road to Sainthood!

A soul's journey is yours to take. In the end, it will be God who sees the path you took!

John Kaufman

SPECIAL THANKS

Informational facts in this publication were, in part, obtained from the worldwide web.

All else are individual singular works of the author John P. Kaufman with all rights reserved.

All written work, poems, and personal information are the sole property of John P. Kaufman.

My special heartfelt thanks to the editing of "Messages From God -The Complicated Road to Sainthood!" Both Ashley Roberts and her mom, Bonnie, worked to help me carefully, and diligently tend to those gaping holes in my sails! The fabric of our sails needs our attention, as do those deep gaping tears in the fabric of our soul.

ABOUT THE AUTHOR

I was born into a family of dairy farmers. I was living in a world, not of my making. Trapped in a place, I could never escape. So many times, I prayed for God to answer my cries of oh lord, why me? Years of living in a cruel, mean, and hateful place had left me mentally ill and suicidal. Then after a lifetime of searching for God's reason for this life of hell on earth, I began to receive subliminal messages. Messages that changed my life forever.

The day I stood before death, witnessed a soul speaking to me above his dead body, what I saw and what he said will leave you like me, believing in God and the eternal soul in us all.